This book belongs to:

First published 2004 by Walker Books Ltd
87 Vauxhall Walk, London SE11 5HJ

This edition published 2005

2 4 6 8 10 9 7 5 3

© 2004 Lucy Cousins
Illustrated in the style of Lucy Cousins by King Rollo Films Ltd

Lucy Cousins font © 2004 Lucy Cousins

The author/illustrator has asserted her moral rights

"Maisy" Audio Visual Series produced by King Rollo Films Ltd
for Universal Pictures International Visual Programming

Maisy™. Maisy is a registered trademark of Walker Books Ltd, London.

Printed in China

British Library Cataloguing in Publication Data:
a catalogue record for this book is
available from the British Library

ISBN-13: 978-1-84428-711-6
ISBN-10: 1-84428-711-4

www.walkerbooks.co.uk

Maisy
Goes Camping

Lucy Cousins

WALKER BOOKS

AND SUBSIDIARIES

LONDON · BOSTON · SYDNEY · AUCKLAND

One summer
afternoon,
Maisy set off
to go camping
in the country.

All her friends went with her.

They found the perfect place to make a camp.

It's hard work pitching a tent.

Oh dear! The tent fell down.
They tried ... and tried ...

and tried again ... until
at last the tent stayed up.

What a big tent!
There's room for everyone.

After supper, they sang songs around the campfire. Then it was time for bed.

First in was Cyril, with his torch.
Nice pyjamas, Cyril!

One
in the
tent!

Next came Charley.
Mind the tent pegs, Charley!

Two in
the tent!

Then it was Tallulah's turn.
Sweet dreams, Tallulah!

Three in the tent!

And make room for Maisy...
Move up, everyone!
Four in the tent!

Is there room for one more? Come on, Eddie!

Oh dear!
Five in the...
(What a
squash!)

Five in the...
(What a
squeeze!)

Five in the... (What a squeezy squish-squash...)

Five in
the tent!

Goodnight,
campers!

POP!
Out popped
Cyril!

POP!
Out
popped
Tallulah!

Sleep tight, campers!

One in the tent...
Four under the stars...

And one in the tree.

Tuwoo!